Text copyright © 2013 by Lou Berger

Illustrations copyright © 2013 by David J. Catrow

All rights reserved. Published in the United States by Schwartz & Wade Books, an imprint
of Random House Children's Books, a division of Random House, Inc., New York.

Schwartz & Wade Books and the colophon are trademarks of Random House, Inc.

Visit us on the Web! randomhouse.com/kids

Educators and librarians, for a variety of teaching tools, visit us at
RHTeachersLibrarians.com

Library of Congress Cataloging-in-Publication Data

Berger, Lou.

Dream dog / Lou Berger ; illustrated by David J. Catrow. — 1st ed.

p. cm.

Summary: Harry cannot have the dog he desperately wants because of his father's
sensitive nose, so he uses his X-35 Infra-Rocket Imagination Helmet to create Waffle,
the dog of his dreams.

ISBN 978-0-375-86655-5 (trade)—ISBN 978-0-375-96655-2 (glb)

[1. Dogs—Fiction. 2. Imagination—Fiction. 3. Fathers and sons—Fiction.]

I. Catrow, David, ill. II. Title.

PZ7.B45213Dre 2013

[E]—dc23

2011048582

The text of this book is set in Aaux Pro.

The illustrations were rendered in gouache, pencil, and ink.

MANUFACTURED IN CHINA

10 9 8 7 6 5 4 3 2 1

First Edition

DREAM DOG

by Lou Berger

illustrated by David Catrow

schwartz & wade books · new york

Harry wanted a dog. No, no, more than wanted! He **wanted** a dog. But Harry's father worked in a pepper factory, and over the years his nose had become twitchy and sensitive, and dogs made him sneeze.

"Please, Dad! A dog, Dad!" begged Harry.

"Sorry, Harry," and "Ya-choo!" said his father.

Harry's father loved him very much, so one day he brought home a pet he hoped would make his son happy. A lizard that changed colors.

The lizard only moved twice a day, and sometimes Harry couldn't see it because it would become the color of his rug or pajamas.

When he took it out to play, it would turn as green as the grass, or as gray as the sidewalk, and once it was almost crushed by Mrs. Kibble's shopping cart.

Harry tried to like the lizard, and he did, a little. He just didn't *love* it. But he had a friend, Mathilda Gold, who looked at it once and loved it deeply.

Harry let her take it home, and Mathilda would gaze into the bathroom mirror with the lizard on her head and watch it turn as red as her hair.

But Harry still wanted a dog.

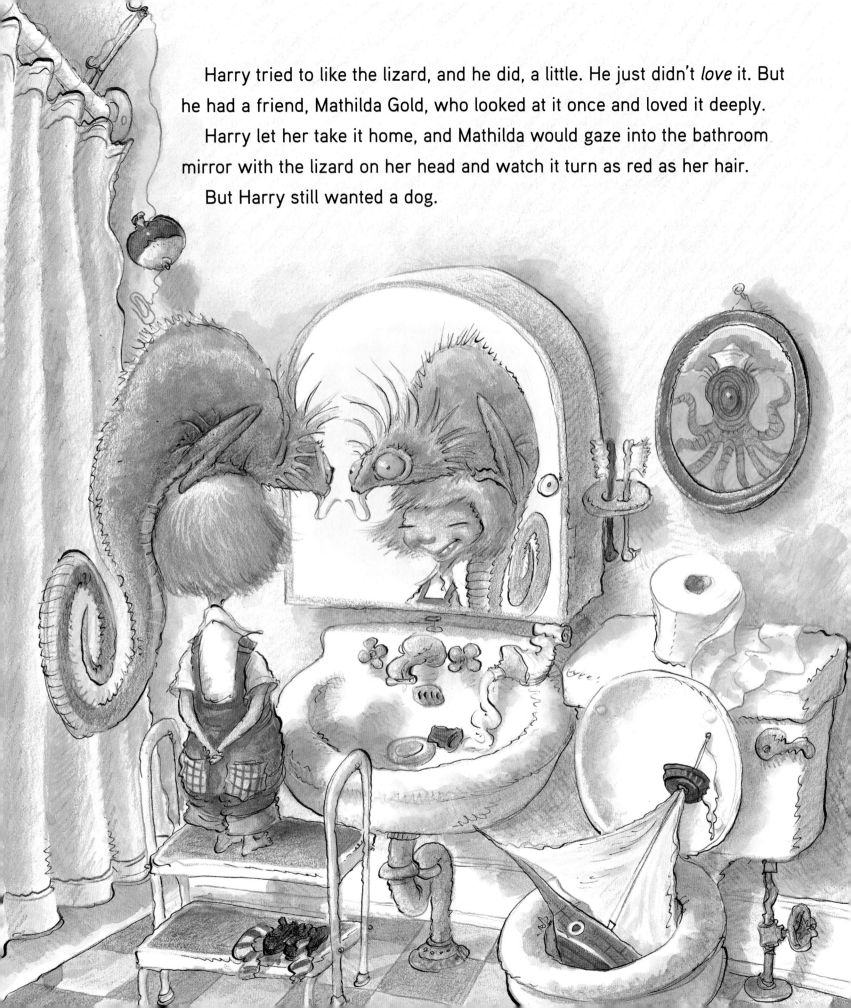

One dogless day, he had an idea.
He would put on his X-35 Infra-Rocket
Imagination Helmet and create a dog
from deep within his own brain.

The X-35 was made out of an old
football helmet, with lots of silvery
aluminum foil that stuck up, zigzagging
like bolts of lightning.

Harry placed it snugly on his
head, sat on his bed, closed his eyes,
and hummed,

Hummmmmmmmm,

and as he hummed,

sommmmmmmething

began to pop into the world.

Paws! A wet nose! An ear! Another
ear! Tail! Tongue! A scruffy body with
three microscopic fleas, and then

Hummmmmmmmmm,

a big friendly head with loving eyes,
and there it was . . .

. . . a dog that looked like all the dogs
that Harry had ever dreamed, and Harry
opened his arms and cried out,

"Waffle!"

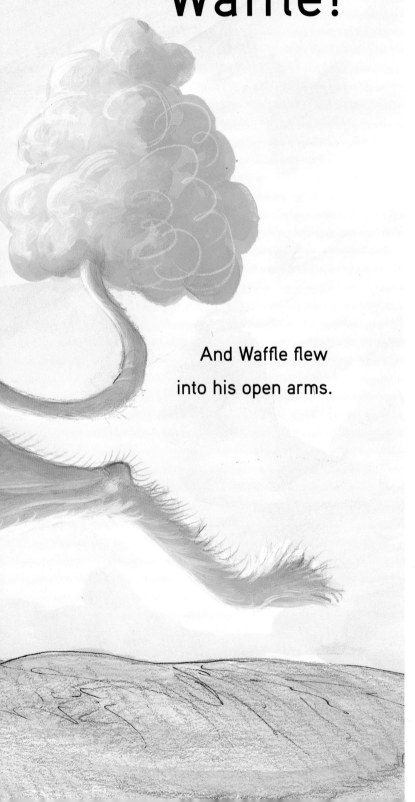

And Waffle flew

into his open arms.

They ran up the stairs
and down the stairs

and all around the park.

From then on, Harry and his dog did everything together. They chased the clouds that scooted across the sky. They played hide-and-seek, and Waffle would scamper deep into the park where Harry couldn't find him. But then Harry would give his special whistle, and Waffle would come bounding out, ears flapping.

At night, Waffle would jump onto Harry's bed and snuggle close, protecting Harry from shadows and creakings.

And when Harry went for a ride in his father's car, Waffle was there too. "Open the window, Dad! Waffle likes to stick his head out and smell everything!"

"Oh," said his father, pushing the button and looking into the rearview mirror.

Harry sometimes used his father's favorite big hairbrush to groom Waffle's fur. "He likes the feel of it," explained Harry. "On his fleas."

"Waffle has fleas?" asked his father.

"Yes. They're hard to see. We might have to give him a shampoo."

"Oh," said his father.

One day, Harry and Waffle were skipping past Mathilda Gold's house. Mathilda was lying on her lawn, the lizard next to her on a piece of blue construction paper. She watched Harry talking to Waffle and said, "That's not a real dog, y'know, Harry."

Harry didn't answer. He just scratched behind Waffle's left ear, because he knew Waffle loved that.

"I can't see him," said Mathilda. "No one can."

"Well, I can hardly see Galileo." Galileo was the name of the lizard.

"That's his natural protection," explained Mathilda. "He takes on the color of the world."

"So does Waffle," said Harry. "He's the color of everything. Fetch, Waffle!" And he threw a stick and Waffle raced after it.

Then something happened at the pepper factory that changed Harry's world. His dad sneezed during a very important meeting—such a stormy sneeze that it blew six pencils, two cups of coffee, nine donuts, and two hundred and forty-seven paper clips off the table. It even blew Mr. Thristle, sitting in his executive-leather swivel chair, fifty-three times around and around. Mr. Thristle was very angry and told Harry's father to leave the pepper factory forever.

One week later, Harry's father found another job, at the local Ping-Pong
ball warehouse.

Moving from pepper to Ping-Pong balls made all the difference to his nose.

Walking home one afternoon, thinking of Harry, his dad wandered into
the Take-Me-Home Animal Shelter. He didn't sneeze.

So on Harry's birthday, his dad brought home a big surprise.

A dog. A real, live dog.

And when this dog saw Harry, it jumped all over him, and Harry could feel its real hot breath, its thick golden fur, and the pounding of its heart.

Now Harry had *two* dogs. He tried to introduce them, but the new dog only looked at Harry, wagging and woofing.

"He can't see Waffle," said his father softly. Then he rubbed Harry's head and left the room.

"Come on," said Harry, "you can see Waffle!"

He pointed to the corner.

"He's right there!

You're a dog!

Can't you smell him?"

"Wroof!"

The dog licked Harry on the forehead.
Harry didn't know what to do. He sat
for a long time on his bed, thinking.

He looked down and saw his X-35 Infra-Rocket Imagination Helmet.

"Yes!" he cried. "This should work."

And he adjusted it on the new dog's head.

Harry twisted the silvery lightning rods and, firmly holding the dog's head, turned it toward Waffle.

"Look over there . . . concentrate . . . *hummmmmmmm.*" Suddenly, the new dog barked.

"Wroof! Wroof!"

Now, Harry's father might have thought the dog was barking at the baby squirrel climbing the tree outside the window, but Harry knew that it was barking at Waffle. And that Waffle was barking back!

"Wroof! Wroof!"

Harry was proud of the new dog, and as he looked into its eyes, he suddenly knew its name.

"Bumper!

You're Bumper!"

Then Harry, Bumper, and Waffle bounded down the stairs, past Harry's father, and out the front door.

They ran down the block and past Mathilda Gold,
who was sitting next to something purple.

They ran past the pepper factory and through the park.
They ran and ran and ran, and played together a long,
long time, until the sun began to set and Waffle suddenly
leaped up into the sky to chase a passing cloud. He looked
like a cloud-dog with misty ears flapping.

Waffle raced after the cloud, woofing
happily . . . and was gone.

Harry was happy that Waffle was happy.

"Come on, Bumper!" he called. "Want to race home?"

Bumper wagged his thick tail.

"Wroof!"